PSYCHOANALYTIC STORIES

PSYCHOANALYTIC STORIES

LUKE HADGE

International Psychoanalytic Books (IPBooks)
New York • http://www.IPBooks.net

Published by International Psychoanalytic Books (IPBooks)
Queens, New York
Online at: www.IPBooks.net

Book cover design by Blackthorn Studio

Interior book design by Medlar Publishing Solutions Pvt Ltd., India

www.IPBooks.net

ISBN: 978-1-949093-43-8

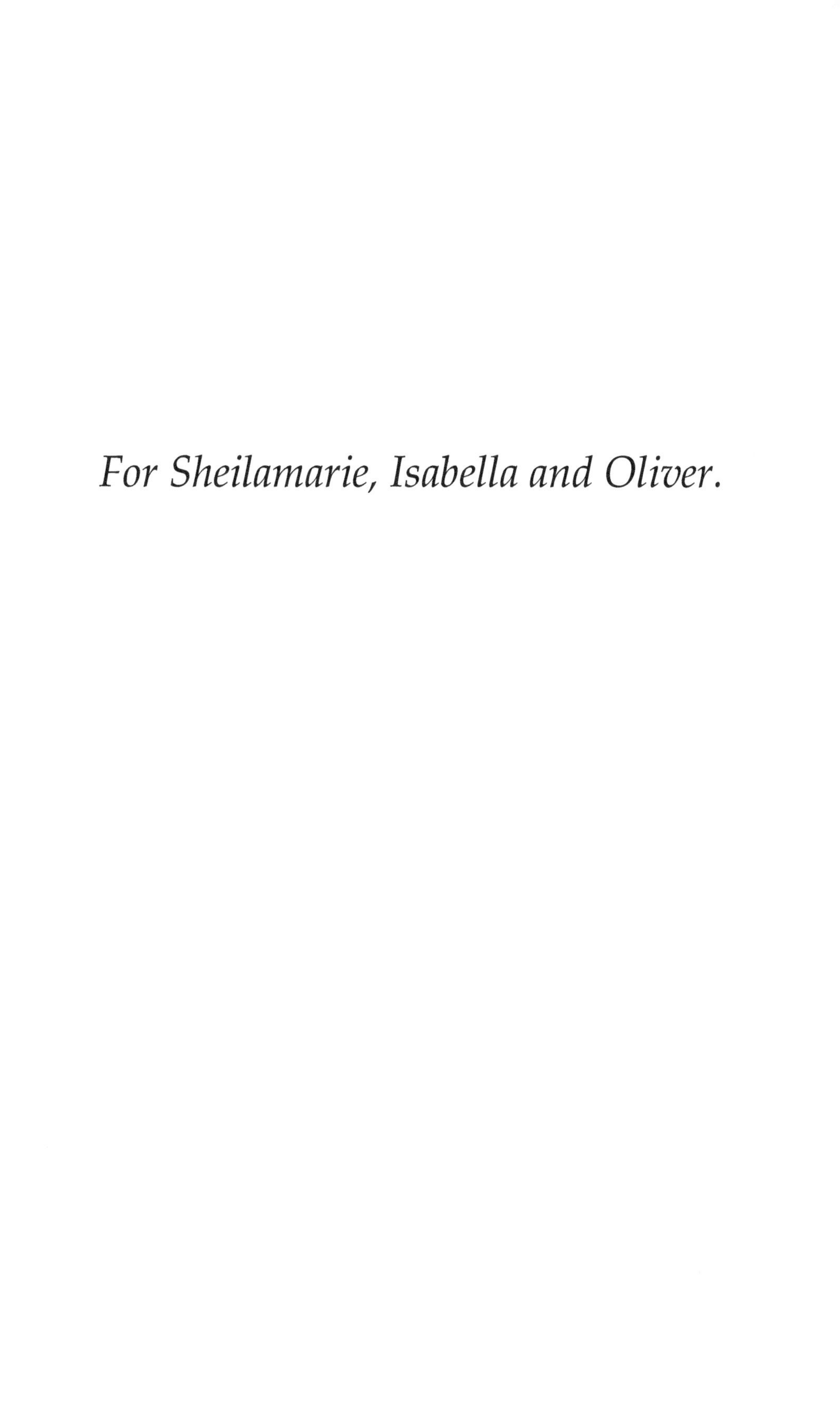

For Sheilamarie, Isabella and Oliver.

TABLE OF CONTENTS

ACKNOWLEDGEMENTS

I would like to thank Warren Poland, Eugene Mahon, Daniel Jacobs, and Ellen Rees for reading and commenting on earlier versions of some of these stories. I would also like to thank Arnold Richards for the publication of this book and Tamar Schwartz at IP Books for her assistance in putting it together. I regret that Morton Aronson is not still around to have seen it.

An earlier version of "The Graduate and the Analyst" was originally published in *The Bulletin of the Association for Psychoanalytic Medicine* and an earlier version of "Jacob Arlow's Office" was originally published in *The American Psychoanalyst*. "Two Charlies on the Subway" is being published simultaneously in this book and in *The Bulletin of the Association for Psychoanalytic Medicine*.

1

THE GRADUATE
AND THE ANALYST

I

You can imagine my surprise when I received a phone call from the famous Dr. Z. Why a senior analyst at Institute X would be calling to request a consultation with a recent graduate was both mysterious and anxiety-provoking. As you know, Dr. Z. was a renowned member of the analytic community for decades, an analyst who made important theoretical and technical contributions to the literature, who was active in various organizations, and, by most accounts, a kind, thoughtful, and magnanimous man who devoted his career to treating patients, teaching, supervising and mentoring students, and writing and presenting papers around the world. His was a distinguished career that any young analyst would admire.

So what could he possibly want with me? When I called him back he was polite but brief, so I agreed to schedule the appointment and have him explain in person.

II

When I think back on the period of time I spent with Dr. Z., I am reminded of the privilege I had working with him. And, in *knowing* him. Although I still wonder from time to time how I might have interpreted something differently to him, or handled certain dynamics in the relationship differently, I cannot forget his expression of gratitude to me when we decided to end the treatment with his reported satisfaction. I did not disagree with him on the matter of terminating; I believed he felt ready to end when he did and that he had completed the piece of work he wished to. He intimated he had something necessary to do next. . . .

Dr. Z. had scaled down his practice and teaching by the time I had started training. I guess you could say he was in the twilight of his career—in age, perhaps, but by no means in creativity. He had been focusing more on writing and less on his long-held commitments to teaching, supervising, administering, etc. I think it was Orson Welles who said that middle age is death for artists and that the greatest creative output is in youth and old age. Perhaps analysts are like artists in this way. Dr. Z.'s writings during this period seemed to be a crystallization of his views on several analytic topics which he had been exploring for many years. Some felt they were among his best works. I sensed that he was disappointed that the institute would no longer let him take candidates for their training analyses because of his advancing age, even though he understood the reasons. I think he also felt rather pushed out of some of the courses he had taught for many years, in favor of candidates' wishes for younger faculty to teach more "contemporary" viewpoints. A number of his close friends and colleagues had passed away as well, leaving him feeling saddened and lonely.

There seemed to be something he wanted to get back in touch with by being back on the couch.

I had been able to take a seminar with Dr. Z. during the early part of my training. Though I might have asked a question or made a comment or two during the course, I hadn't expected to have made any impression on him, least of all one strong enough for him to contact me later on with his most unusual request. Heaven knows how little I really understood about psychoanalysis at that time.

As he sat in my office that fateful first meeting, I wondered if I was making a Faustian bargain. He did most of the talking; I listened. Naturally, he provided relevant history and background. He framed the issue he was facing in a somewhat vague manner, it seemed to me. I couldn't quite put my finger on the problem. I told him so and he said: "Yes, I know." He offered further associations and even some dream material. Clearly, he knew how to conduct the first encounter. He was a good patient right from the beginning. Still, in his story there was something unclear.

I wondered: Was he having a crisis, at this time in his life, in his faith in psychoanalysis? Was he afraid he had gotten something terribly wrong in one of his analytic ideas? Was there some old neurotic ghost visiting him again? Was he terrified of his mortality? Did he desperately not want to be deprived of practicing—and *experiencing*—more analysis?

III

Things have a strange way of working themselves out sometimes, or not. Dr. Z. was offering an opportunity which stimulated certain anxieties in me with which I had to grapple. As a recent graduate, I did not quite feel comfortable analyzing someone as senior and superior to me in experience and expertise. You could say I had some misgivings. My associations went to the opening sentence in W. Somerset Maugham's *The Razor's Edge*, a novel I read in my youth: "I have never begun a novel with more misgiving." *I had never begun an analysis with more misgiving.* Perhaps it was my own insecurity after having recently graduated and entered the post-graduate phase, when consolidation of one's analytic identity is thought to take place. Looking back on it I wonder how "free" I was in my choice to treat Dr. Z. at the time. How could I say no to him? But then I realized: I didn't have to say no. I could say yes. It was my own neurotic ghost I had to confront, my own razor's edge to negotiate.

In addition, Dr. Z. understandably did not want me to write about him or refer to any content of our work while he was alive. Yet, he left open the possibility for me to write about him and the treatment in some capacity after he had died, using my own discretion. However, I almost felt like Max Brod to his Kafka (an author, it turned out, he admired), when Dr. Z. entrusted me with his papers on the condition that I promise to burn them all after his death. I think he left it purposely up to me, so that I would have to use my own judgment and honor his legacy, as I saw fit. Thus the analysis began.

An opportunity for a recent graduate to analyze a senior analyst? That doesn't come along every day. In fact, our field is perpetuated by the near opposite: Training analysts analyzing candidates. In a sense, my treating Dr. Z. was a reversal with profound meanings. I could see how this relationship gratified a displaced transference wish from my own analysis. I had felt cared for and understood and I wanted to return the favor. Maybe I even had the fantasy of knowing my former training analyst better, of being able to analyze him, by analyzing Dr. Z.

Being tempted to rework the system, to enter unchartered territory, to engage in a unique pact—all these interpretations, however, yielded to a greater pleasure: To immerse myself in Dr. Z.'s mind.

And here's the rub: What I would find there could make or break me as an analyst. I hoped to understand him at a deep level and his unconscious mind both intrigued and frightened me. It was a vast place, with nooks and crannies, hidden corners, expansive vistas, even culs de sac. It was easy to get lost in it. It was active and alive, always at work. But would there be something there I did not want to find, would not want to know? Something about this great analyst that would shatter my admiration of him? Something unsavory about the field in which I was entering? Something about him that I would become? Fear of my own demise? There was some vague (that word again) foreboding I could not articulate. Something like the feeling in Henry James's "The Beast in The Jungle," a story which my father gave me to read as a child. There is something lurking out there—or rather, *in here*. For James, for Dr. Z., I believe, and then for me, it remained ever-present and unknowable: The beast in the jungle within us.

I wondered if that beast, for Dr. Z., was his awareness of his impending mortality. A lifetime of work and study, family and love. A career of analytic thought and practice. Was his life of the mind now a fear of death? And did I represent some aspect of his past youthful self, entering into the door that was now closing on him? Did he wish to pass down something to me? Was it my own rite of passage to analyze him?

Was Dr. Z. at that stage when he was looking back and wanting to understand something about his life, as he wore the bottoms of his trousers rolled, like T. S. Eliot's J. Alfred Prufrock, whom he often quoted? Was he taking stock, reassessing, reconciling? Where was the conflict? Here was a man who thought deeply about things; his writings and lectures attested to this. But now he was on my couch and I could see for myself the depth. I could see that the beast in the jungle exists even for the psychoanalyst, and maybe even more so.

In one session he recalled a long-forgotten memory, one he had only told to his own training analyst. As a kid, he used to walk the streets of Manhattan thinking to himself: "O God, let me think deep thoughts while walking down the street." What did this mean?

In another session, his associations led him to say, tongue-in-cheek, what I heard as the most subversive idea in all my training, aside, of course, from the very idea of analysis itself: "Maybe every graduate should analyze a senior analyst." He meant this for the benefit of the junior analyst, but perhaps both young and old could learn from and enrich each other.

Dr. Z. occasionally associated to some of the current controversies and debates roiling the field. He was genuinely concerned and upset about the state of things: The internal fights, the factions, the lack of respect in the scientific community, the dwindling number of patients interested in analytic treatment, what he thought were declining standards, and his feeling that the field was moving away from something fundamentally important to his understanding of psychoanalysis. However, at one point in these reflections, he said somewhat mournfully: "But I guess psychoanalysis is for the young people now to make of it what they want." I wondered if that included me.

The sessions with him often had a surreal quality—was it a shared reverie? I tried to throw the theory I had learned to the winds, but theory kept rearing its clever head. I tried to listen with "evenly hovering attention." I tried to listen "without memory or desire." At times, I tried to see if I could consciously not listen. But he drew me back in. I found myself forgetting I was I and he was he. At times I felt he had achieved an almost advanced level of free association. I don't know how to describe this, except a free association bordering on *silence*. Perhaps seasoned analysts can do this. Deep in the analytic hour I tried to let Dr. Z.'s mind wash over me.

- The more I was analyzing Dr. Z., the more he was analyzing me.
- The more he was analyzing me, the more I was analyzing myself.
- I told myself: *Always be analyzing . . .*

IV

When I think back on what I learned from my classes, my control cases and supervision, and my own analysis, I must also include the brief—and interminable—time with Dr. Z. as one of the most rewarding, and curious, parts of my training and post-graduate experience. A strange interlude, the meaning of which I am still trying to understand. An analysis—strange, difficult, and wonderful. Perhaps he wanted it that way, planned it like that for me. It was his last *analytic function* which left in me a powerful identification.

Now, after his leaving and upon my reflection, I carry on and Dr. Z. is a part of me as I struggle with something about his struggle. And when I am deep in the analytic hour with a patient or walking the streets in this mad city trying to think, I still try to let Dr. Z.'s mind wash over me, and tell myself to always be analyzing, like him to the end, and remember that moment in the final hour when he said, "Everything is interesting if you look deeply enough."

2

Jacob Arlow's Office

Some years ago, I rented an office in a suite that included the office Jacob Arlow used for many years. This was on the ground floor of a residential building in the Murray Hill neighborhood of Manhattan. I had just started psychoanalytic training when I found the office and thought it an amusing coincidence when I learned that Arlow used to practice in the suite, since I assumed I would be reading some of Arlow's work during training. The owner of the suite, herself an analyst, used Arlow's actual office and had been the person who told me who the former occupant had been when I visited the suite originally.

I remained in the suite for the duration of my analytic training and often thought about Arlow having worked in that space. A couple of times when repairs were being made to my office, my suitemate let me use her office, Arlow's old room. There was nothing particularly striking about this room. It was actually smaller than mine. It had a rectangular shape and the dimensions were probably about 20' by 12' with windows on two perpendicular walls, one of which looked out into the building's backyard, as did my own office. The backyard was quite lovely, consisting of a small grassy area and a row of large trees. The top of the Empire State Building could be seen in the distance. The trees in the backyard attracted a variety of birds, not just pigeons, who frequently sang their songs while all of us worked in the suite. My ignorance of fowls showed when I thought I was hearing the sounds of owls. I asked myself, why would owls be perched outside analysts' offices in New York City? Someone eventually enlightened me that they were probably mourning doves (perhaps a more appropriate bird for analysts). I often sat in my chair during breaks between patients and let my gaze drift out into the backyard, followed by my thoughts. I wondered if Arlow allowed himself such brief reveries looking out the window during long days of analytic work.

My landlord also informed me when I moved in that just over the other side of the trees in the backyard was the townhouse where the writer Salman Rushdie lived. It was a grand townhouse and sometimes when I worked late into the evening I could see lights on in the rooms in the back of the building. I wondered if the famous author was in there writing. In addition to *Midnight's Children*, how about *Midnight's Analyst*? One day while I was bringing back to my office a pastrami sandwich for lunch, I walked past Rushdie on the street corner hailing a taxi. Where was he going? This was years after the Iranian government dropped its support of the *fatwa* issued for *The Satanic Verses* in 1988, so he certainly could move around more freely. But I still wondered if he feared for his safety—the *fatwa* actually remained in place—and what it must have been like to live under a death threat.

We all live under a certain kind of *fatwa*, not imposed by an ayatollah, but by life itself. And how we deal with it, or what we do with this constant internal threat is one aspect that can be extrapolated from Freud's concept of the "death instinct."

Rushdie recently published a memoir, *Joseph Anton*, about his experience of living under such a concrete or external death threat. The *fatwa* did not stop Rushdie from writing, but it did engender much upheaval to his personal life. Denial is one powerful weapon against the ever-present reality of death. In a darkly humorous example of this, during the years I worked in Arlow's former suite, mail was still delivered to him, five to ten years after he had died in 2004. Much of it was junk mail. But on more than one occasion he received notices for upcoming psychoanalytic lectures and conferences. I thought, "Don't people know he's dead and that they should take him off their mailing lists?" One particular flier addressed to him caught my attention. It was from an institute in the city advertising a conference called "Psychoanalysis and Art: Dialogues in the Creative Process." Arlow's interest in art and creativity apparently extended beyond the grave. Among the billed speakers were Harold Blum, Rosalind Krauss, and Joseph Lichtenberg. I took some measure of comfort in the belief that analysts, alive and dead, still try to communicate with each other in the spirit of sharing ideas and passing on psychoanalytic knowledge.

But aside from the occasional piece of mail, I found myself wondering if there was anything else in the suite that belonged to Arlow. Could any of his belongings or personal effects have been left behind? Would I find something in the closets or the kitchen cabinet? Notes on a case? An unpublished paper? A beloved tchotchke? I felt the urge to poke around in the hope of discovering something of Arlow's, almost as if I were a child again snooping in my parents' bedroom. Though I restrained the impulse to enact this fantasy, I imagined there still might be something of his hidden, or buried, somewhere in the suite.

During this period, I attended an informative lecture given by Michelle Press discussing Arlow's classic 1969 paper,

"Unconscious Fantasies and Disturbances of Conscious Experience." It was held at the New York Psychoanalytic Society, Arlow's institute, where he served as president in the 1960s. I was struck in this paper by Arlow's examination of the ubiquity and significance of unconscious fantasy. A dramatic example of this occurred with my office playing a major role. Shortly after I graduated from training, I was still treating in analysis one of my former control cases, a woman with a serious alcohol problem. One day when I was not working she showed up at my suite intoxicated and tried to break into my office so she could "sleep it off" on my couch. She damaged my office door but was unable to enter the room. She proceeded to lie down on the chairs in the waiting room. My suitemate insisted several times that she needed to leave and my patient eventually departed only after my colleague threatened to call the police. She wanted to be in my space, on my couch, in my room, even if I wasn't there. We came to later understand that in her regressed state she wanted to return to the safe "holding environment" of my office and in her unconscious fantasy be close to me.

Arlow died several years before I started working in his former "space." The idea of space, physical and psychic, and who occupies it, like Rushdie's living space, Arlow's former workspace, or my new workspace, came to take on new meanings, conscious and unconscious, for me. I don't know what Arlow's office looked like when he worked in it. I imagine it was full of books, journals, some artwork—what most analysts have in their offices. But Arlow made important contributions to the field of psychoanalysis while sitting in that office. It occurred to me he probably had written some of his best papers right next door to me. I could imagine him sitting in there working out thoughts and ideas in his mind or listening to patients in his analytic way, as I was learning how to do in my own analytic way as well. Of course, this is my fantasy. And fantasy was a major area of interest for Arlow. So it has been for Rushdie, too. In fact, much of the material deemed so offensive to Muslims in Rushdie's *The Satanic Verses* was "dream visions" and narrative informed by magic realism, which were largely responsible for his being issued the *fatwa*. One artist's creative fantasy is another reader's unacceptable blasphemy. Did Arlow and Rushdie know they lived and worked across the backyard from each other? Did they ever see each other in the neighborhood? Did they read each other?

So I fantasized about Arlow working in his office. I wonder how many analysts know who occupied their offices before them. Generations of analysts have worked in the same rooms. The anthropological history of such workspaces stimulates further fantasies and associations. My own associations to offices, or rooms, as depicted in famous titles of art and literature, include Virginia Woolf's *Jacob's Room* (Arlow's office?); James Baldwin's *Giovanni's Room*; Truman Capote's evocative title, *Other Voices, Other Rooms*; one of my favorite Van Gogh paintings, "Bedroom in Arles" (how did he live and work in that room?); or the benefit of having, in E. M. Forster's words, *A Room with a View*, and in Woolf's words, *A Room of One's Own*. And, of course, Freud's consulting room at Berggasse 19, in Vienna, perhaps the most famous office in history. If not, certainly one of the most discussed and photographed workspaces in any discipline in any era. Edmund Engleman's *Berggasse 19: Sigmund Freud's Home and Offices, Vienna 1938* documents in images one person's quarters like no other attempt I know. There have been more recent efforts to write about and photograph contemporary analysts' offices, including Mark Gerald's 2011 paper, "The Past, Present, and Future," and Sebastian Zimmermann's 2014 book *Fifty Shrinks*, which shows the interiors of 50 therapists' and analysts' offices around the world.

Then I think about all the offices I have worked in both in my practice and also in hospitals and clinics over the years. How much time I've spent in these little rooms, sitting with another person, listening, talking, looking, thinking. We spend so much of our working, and waking, life in the relatively small confines of rooms of our own with a view outward and hopefully inward. With our books, papers, artwork, objects internal and external, mementos mori, pads and pens. The enclosed space is contrasted with the infinite regions of the minds we attempt to explore of our patients and ourselves.

T.S. Eliot wrote at the end of "The Love Song of J. Alfred Prufrock," "We have lingered in the chambers of the sea." I sometimes feel this is an apt metaphor—another Arlow interest—for our experience in our offices with our patients day in and day out, hour after hour, depth upon depth. "Till human voices wake us, and we drown."

It is some small consolation to suspect that, like Arlow, we all may well continue to receive mail long after we're gone.

3

Two Charlies
on the Subway

It was the strangest pick-up line I ever heard.

"I used to *know* Charlie Brenner."

The well-dressed, mild-mannered elderly man had leaned over toward me and spoke in a warm, disarming tone, and his line immediately grabbed my interest. For I was sitting in the middle of a subway car in Manhattan reading *An Elementary Textbook of Psychoanalysis*, written by none other than Charles Brenner. My curiosity piqued, I turned to him and replied, "Oh?" The dapper gentleman inched closer to me and explained how years ago he had worked as an administrator of a mental health agency in New York City where Dr. Brenner served as a consultant. During this period, he added, he had gotten to know him fairly well and respected him greatly.

He then asked me why I was reading Brenner's book. I told him that I was working at a mental health clinic and that I was interested in psychoanalysis. I asked him if he still worked in mental health care and he answered no, he currently was in the art world running a foundation which gave grants to young artists. As the train was approaching my station I told him I had to get off and that it was nice to meet him. He handed me his business card and invited me to call him sometime. His name, it turned out, was Charles too.

Though this incident occurred over a quarter-century ago, I recall it fondly with a mixture of nostalgia, humor, and sadness. This man, Charles Bergman,—Charlie, to me—died this past year, and Charles Brenner, of course, has been dead for ten years now. Long gone too is my youthful 20-something self sitting in the pre-smartphone, pre-overcrowded subway reading about psychoanalysis with its seeds being planted in my mind for a future career. I was a psychology major fresh out of college heading downtown to lower Manhattan to my first real job. I was a "utilization reviewer," which meant, unglamorously, that I read patient charts. All day. Every day. For anyone who has practiced psychotherapy at an outpatient clinic and received annoying notices about unsigned progress notes, tardy treatment plans, or incomplete termination summaries, I was one of those nameless authorial villains. I don't know if agencies still employ such URs, but for over a year in the early 1990s, I buried myself in thick records, sitting in the poorly ventilated records room battling tedium, bureaucratic regulations, and poor handwriting. Nevertheless, it was my first exposure to working in the mental health—or, rather, mental illness—world. And, in all honesty, I enjoyed much of it. I was privileged to read about real patients suffering from real mental illness and how they were being treated—cared for—by dedicated therapists and psychiatrists in a community-oriented setting. I also got to meet and talk with staff, some of whom took an interest in this young guy sitting in the records room all day who showed a burgeoning curiosity about psychotherapy and psychoanalysis. This agency also had a well-respected psychology internship and an analytic training program, mostly for non-MDs, so I'm not sure Charles Brenner would have approved at that time. My employment, nevertheless, was highlighted not least of all by at least one enduring friendship with a staff psychologist who, early in my tenure, one day asked me deadpan, "What the hell do you do here?" "I read charts," I replied. And thus began a friendship which lasted until this past year when he too died, far too young in his 50s from ALS.

Since the clinic was analytically oriented, the intake process for new patients utilized measures intended to offer dynamic insights about the patients. Personality and projective testing—heaven forbid!—was often completed. In addition, a measure called the "Early Memories Test," by the psychologist Martin Mayman (who happened to have been one of the doctoral professors of my new psychologist friend at the clinic) was often administered as part of the evaluation process. This "test" asked the respondent to recall early memories of self and of important people, such as mother and father. I will never forget one patient's answer. Asked to describe her earliest memory in life, this woman in her sixties stated, "I remember my birth trauma." I was dumbfounded. This could be a *real* memory? Was this possible? I was incredulous: It must be a *fantasy*. I didn't know if this patient had read any Otto Rank or if she understood her "birth trauma" memory the way Rank tried to theorize about "the trauma of birth" and resultant anxiety and neuroses. But her answer haunted me for years and I came to think maybe it didn't actually matter if it was a true memory, or a screen memory (of what? imagine that!), or an unconscious fantasy, or a conscious fantasy, because this was a traumatized space in her intrapsychic world, she believed it, and it formed a narrative which informed her life, as I read on. . . .

It was with my new friend that I attended a lecture at Brenner's institute, New York Psychoanalytic Society and Institute, in the mid 1990s, when I spotted Brenner, tall and stately, walking down the aisle to his seat holding hands with his wife. "Look at that," I said to my friend, "Brenner must be in his eighties and he's still coming to psychoanalytic meetings and holding his wife's hand!" "Maybe he needs his wife's support to walk," my friend opined. I wanted to tell Brenner that I had read his book on the subway, but I wasn't sure how he would take that.

Charles Brenner lived till 94 and Charles Bergman lived till 84. Full lives engaged in their work till close to the end. They both left substantial legacies in their respective fields. The foundation Bergman headed for many years, the Pollock-Krasner Foundation, named for Jackson Pollock and Lee Krasner, is still going strong, providing financial support to artists of "recognizable artistic merit and demonstrable financial need," as its mission states. Brenner's legacy seems a bit more complicated these days, however. When I was involved in my own analytic training, just ten years ago, around the time Brenner passed away, I was surprised how little of Brenner we read as candidates. Brenner, once a leading figure for decades in American psychoanalysis, had, at least in my training, been relegated to a more supporting role, if that. References to his work were receding as well in the literature we read in classes.

It's interesting how some prominent psychoanalytic thinkers become passé, or marginalized, or outright ostracized, for certain periods, for certain reasons, only to be "re-discovered" by later generations. Ferenczi certainly comes to mind in this regard, as does Bowlby. Perhaps psychoanalytic thought nearing 2020 now has moved well beyond Brenner's psychic *weltanschauung*, but, for me, it was still reading his *Elementary Textbook* on the subway which lit a fire and led me back to reading Freud, which has stoked it ever since.

So I had to give this nice old man Charlie Bergman a call, after all: Both to make another new friend and learn about the art world *and* to learn more about Charlie Brenner and psychoanalysis. Charlie and I had lunch; he took me to a swanky bistro in midtown where we sat outside and sipped wine in the afternoon sunlight. He asked me what my aspirations were. He told me about his work at the foundation and his eclectic career before. He shared his positive memories of Brenner.

Another time we watched early returns come in during the 1992 presidential election, when Bill Clinton defeated George Bush pere, who, as it happens, died this past year as well. Charlie had much interest in politics. He had, in fact, been politically involved earlier in his career, having served as an advisor to Presidents Nixon, Ford, and Carter on issues related to mental health. Clearly, he had a distinguished professional career and, I would find out, an interesting personal life. He had had a number of romances, including, he told me, a secret affair with a prominent politician. I must admit, with some embarrassment, that, at the time, I was not that familiar with this politician, so I had to look him up—a much harder task in those pre-Wikipedia days!

Since I was straight, our relationship was a friendship. Come to think of it, after all these years, perhaps I misinterpreted his introductory appeal to start with. Perhaps in those days in my youth I read sex into everything, saw sex everywhere. (Maybe Brenner would have been pleased with my preoccupation with sex!) He seemed to take a genuine interest in me and in my genuine interests, which, aside from my own heterosexual pick-up lines, were psychology, psychoanalysis, the arts, and other, I fancied, intellectual endeavors.

On another occasion, he introduced me to another young man, displaying similar sartorial splendor, with whom he thought I would get along well. All three of us had lunch together one time, and I remember to this day what felt like then stimulating conversation.

But then I finally got my act together and graduated from the clinic records room to start graduate school proper. I become immersed in my psychology studies and started working as a psychotherapy trainee in a clinic, writing my own progress notes, treatment plans, and termination summaries. And, getting my own correspondences from "utilization reviewers." Being on the other side felt both rewarding and, well, annoying too. Alas, I lost touch with Charlie and he with me. . . .

Almost 30 years later, I re-read Brenner's *Elementary Textbook* —on the subway, again. Viewed through a contemporary lens the book, published in 1955, reads like a relic from a distant psychoanalytic past. Maybe this is not such a bad thing, for it shows how far psychoanalysis has come. However, at the same time, I happen to think that Brenner's work still matters, as part of the foundation of ever-evolving psychoanalytic thought, as part of the core of a still relevant and vital school of analytic theory and practice, and as a faithful exegesis of much of Freud's major discoveries. "Every thinker/is a piece of the continent, a part of the main;" to paraphrase the poet John Donne. Yet, in *Elementary Textbook*, which, astonishingly, has sold well over a million copies, Brenner is clear about what he believes "psychoanalysis" is—a definitional effort still useful, to my mind, in today's pluralistic theoretical landscape, whether one agrees or not.

What Brenner believed psychoanalysis to be and not to be is brought home with reflective clarity in his final published paper, an insightful and refreshingly candid personal essay, titled "Memoir," published posthumously in 2009, a year after he died. Perhaps it was only that late in his life that he could write as honestly and as self-deprecatingly as he did about his own *bildungsroman*, no less as forcefully about his analytic beliefs. To bear the dead a benefit of the doubt, I reserve a modicum of leniency for what reads as some of Brenner's biases by remembering he was a man of a particular era, that is, a certain time and place and culture. The same can and has been said, of course, about some of Freud's questionable patriarchal prejudices which may have infiltrated his theorizing.

Be that as it may, what a delight it was to read in his "Memoir" that he actually wrote in long-hand the first draft of *Elementary Textbook* on the train! In his case it was the daily commuter train from his home in Westchester to his office in Manhattan, and back, in those pre-computer days. Thus the rail train ride of my own "memoir" comes full circle. . . .

So I became an analyst and embarked on an analytic career in my own way and, like Brenner reminisces, for my own reasons. And I remember reading a slim volume on something called psychoanalysis on the subway some 360 full moons ago when a chance encounter would burnish a memory and paint a subsequent canvas of associations. As a saying should say, "You never know whom you might meet on a New York City subway." On another day, at another time, perhaps on the same subway line, as luck would have it, I might have been reading the brochure of the Pollock-Krasner Foundation, two artists who later became of interest to me, and an aged, dapper, and similarly mischievous Charles Brenner might have leaned over to me and whispered, "I used to *know* Charlie Bergman."

4

THE SALMAN RUSHDIE BIRD

When I rented my first full-time private office in New York City, the landlord told me that Salman Rushdie lived in one of the houses on the other side of the backyard garden. My office was in the back of a building and it faced a little garden shared by the other tenants of the offices on the ground floor. The garden was lined with trees and visited by different kinds of birds from time to time. On the other side of the garden were the backs of a row of elegant townhouses and brownstones. As the landlord was helping me get settled into the office one day she pointed to one of townhouses and said that Rushdie lived there. Then she said, "But don't tell anyone." I asked, "Why, isn't the *fatwa* over?" She said it was but that he still probably wouldn't want a lot of people to know he lived there. The landlord, apparently an avid Rushdie follower, said further that a couple of times she had looked out of her window and saw him, his back to his window, sitting in a bathrobe at his desk writing.

I left that conversation wondering why she had instructed me to not tell anyone. Was Rushdie still concerned about his freedom? What was I going to do, leak it to the gossip pages of the local tabloids? "Famous author writes in his bathrobe"? I certainly wasn't going to inform my patients that a famous writer lived across the garden, although I did indulge in the fantasy that I could market my new psychoanalytic practice with the enticement of possible Rushdie sightings. It was hard enough trying to engage patients to undergo as an intensive, lengthy and expensive treatment as psychoanalysis; any added incentive was worth considering. Nevertheless, the idea of a "Rushdie sighting" got planted in my mind and I have to admit that oftentimes during the subsequent months I found myself looking around as I went in and out of my building or walked in the neighborhood. In addition, at the beginning or end of each day, as I opened or closed the blinds in my office, I glanced out of the window to his townhouse to see if I could see him, possibly at his desk writing, or looking out of his window too at the back of my building or at the birds in the garden.

There's an old Leonard Cohen song called "Bird on the Wire," that I used to listen to, which includes the lyrics:

"Like a bird on the wire
Like a drunk in a midnight choir
I have tried in my way to be free"

Life, schooling, and other authors, had gotten in the way of my reading more of Rushdie's writing over the years leading up to my new office. Meanwhile for him, his writing was his life and could have been his death. So I felt it incumbent upon me to read more of my new neighbor. During the years I worked in that office, I worked my way through his novels, often reading chapters in between patient sessions. Up to that point, the closest connection I had had to Rushdie was a girlfriend in graduate school—in another big city and what feels like many moons ago.

She was of Indian descent and Rushdie was her favorite writer. As we were spending more time together and our relationship was deepening, often by taking long walks and talking, she suggested one day we give each other our favorite short story to read. Her thinking was that our favorite story would reflect something about ourselves, and thereby we would understand each other better by sharing this. I had a hard time deciding what my favorite story was; I could think of many favorite stories. I protested to her; but to no avail, she insisted on my choosing just one. Up against the wall, I decided upon Chekhov's "The Bet." I remembered that I had read this story in my youth and I had been very taken with it. The idea that a man, on a bet, would willingly lock himself up for ten years in total isolation from the outside world and have no human contact, was somehow both unthinkable and yet alluring to me. The fact that the only condition he requested was to be provided with books to read—scores of them over the years covering any topic of his choosing—made the conceit even more fascinating. Imagine that: Nothing to do for ten years but read! The ending of the story—the decision he makes—knocked me out.

When my girlfriend and I exchanged stories, I, supercilious, thought to myself: "Rushdie? Of all the great short stories and short story writers, you choose this one? Sorry, Rushdie's OK, but he is no Chekov." She had chosen Rushdie's "The Courter." Be that as it may, I took her paperback edition of Rushdie's stories, *East, West* and gave her my father's old Library of America hardcover edition of *Great Russian Short Stories*, which I had been safekeeping, which included Chekhov, Tolstoy, Dostoevsky, Gogol, Pushkin. I was worried I might not get my book back.

So that night I read Rushdie's "The Courter." In all honesty, I was disappointed. Perhaps it was because I was expecting to be disappointed, that I was. I just felt, how could this compare to "The Bet"? I thought "The Courter" was a nice, somewhat sad story, and I thought what a terrible thing to have felt that a story was "nice." Conversely, I still thought "The Bet" was devastating. I was at an age and place in life when I read something—and something not in my dry field of study but rather "literature"—I wanted to be devastated. I wanted a story either in its subject matter or its style to shake my foundation; when I had read "The Bet" as an adolescent it had done exactly that. When I read it again, it still held such power for me. In my darker, moodier moments in graduate school, before I had met this young woman who was full of life and hope, I was hung up on Leonard Cohen songs, the ones about loneliness, loss, and forbidden desire: The haunting, brooding songs, like the brooding, thick and dense Russian stories.

However, just because "The Bet" had affected me in that way didn't mean it would someone else. Someone from the other gender, from a different culture, from a different life experience, and certainly with different tastes and sensibilities. I had misread this woman and foolishly wanted her to be similarly moved by "my story" as I was. At the same time, I was not open to understanding "her story" as much as I should have been in order to understand *her*.

Nevertheless, at the time I thought we had a reasonably interesting discussion about both stories, though only in retrospect did I realize that she must have picked up on my less-than-enthusiastic response to or my interpretation of "The Courter." I don't remember her showing it overtly, but I think something changed for her then about our relationship. Sometime later, she made the comment to me: "Don't you think we're very different." Despite my responding, "I think our differences are very similar," the humor was lost by that point. And, alas, so was the relationship.

"*I have tried in my way to be free*," echoed broodingly in my mind again, after we broke up.

Ten years later: One night I was working late in my new office, writing patient notes, when I looked up from my desk and saw a light on in one of the back rooms in the Rushdie residence across the garden. I wondered if he was at his desk too working late. Maybe writing something that would offend somebody somewhere, put another price on his head, cause him to lose his freedom again. Was writing worth that? Another ten years in isolation, *against* your will unlike the Chekhov character, until things change again in the world, until someone says, "Enough! What does it matter what Rushdie writes?" And the world moves on to more pressing matters?

Months passed. Then something peculiar happened. One afternoon my analysand was lying on the couch free-associating. I was sitting in my chair behind him and I think I fell into a reverie: I was listening to my patient but I was also not listening. Actually, I think I was listening unconsciously, the way Bion talked about a mother's mind capturing the infant's mind. Consciously my mind was drifting. I was staring out of the window in this altered state and all of a sudden a little bird alighted on a branch of the tree outside of my window. Immediately, instinctively—out of my unconscious—I blurted to myself "Salman Rushdie!" In that split-second moment I thought the bird was Rushdie. There he was!

Just as quickly I came to my senses and realized it wasn't Rushdie; it was just a bird. A little multi-colored feathered bird, the species of which I had no idea, just minding its own business sitting on a tree branch. Looking around itself. It remained there for a minute or two; I couldn't say for sure as my sense of time was disoriented. Then out of somewhere, *bird-on-the-branch* became *bird-on-the-wire* and I instantly heard in my mind the bird sing, *"I have tried in my way to be free."* Then the bird flew away. How curious!

I realigned my conscious awareness to my patient's speech and understood that he had been talking about how he was trying to extricate himself from his fears and inhibitions. He wanted to feel more independent in his life, be more creative, not be afraid to put himself out in the world. He wanted to liberate himself from years of a kind of self-imposed isolation, hiding, and paralysis. He was trying to face himself and create a new life. He was trying in his way to be free.

Another ten years passed and I decided to read Salman Rushdie's "The Courter" again. It was not the same story I had read twenty years before; nor was I the same person I was twenty years ago. I am not with my graduate-school girlfriend anymore. I am here and she is, I don't know, somewhere else. Perhaps back in India. She exists in my mind as a lost love. *A sweet bird of youth.* Would she still choose "The Courter" as her favorite story? Would I still choose Chekhov's "The Bet"? Twenty years later Rushdie has written a memoir about his years in hiding under the *fatwa*, titled *Joseph Anton*, the pseudonym he used to disguise his identity, a name representing Joseph Conrad *and* Anton Chekhov, his two favorite writers. Has Rushdie read Chekhov's "The Bet"? Did he read it during his hiding? If Leonard Cohen was still alive would he still sing of a bird being free? What happened to that bird outside my office window? Has my patient found the freedom he so wished for?

Why we exchanged those stories so many years ago demanded new reflection. Did she choose "The Courter" because she was thinking that she was like the Certainly-Mary character and I was like the Mixed-Up courter character? Wasn't the narrator of the story Rushdie himself and that she too, like him, struggled with a tension between being separated from her homeland, India, and living in a foreign country? Did she know that she might need to return home, like Certainly-Mary? Maybe she didn't know this yet on a conscious level but was communicating to me her unconscious wish to return home, which would mean we would have to part. Was she trying to tell me that she didn't think that our love would last? That I was too *mixed-up*? That our love was like a bird flitting on a branch for a moment, then it flies away? Did I choose "The Bet" because I was trying to tell her something about myself that I wasn't aware of? Was I trying to show her another side of me: The antisocial or schizoid side of me that would like to be shut away from humanity for years with only books to keep me company? That I was more engaged with books than people? That I was incapable of really loving her?

I had been wrong about her and I had been wrong about Rushdie's story. It's a far richer and deeper story than I had appreciated at the time, because it hadn't occurred to me then to consider the possible latent meanings of who the characters represented and where the story was heading. We were all in the story: Myself, my girlfriend, the desire for love and the wish to be free, with Rushdie himself reflecting back on his childhood. With a devastating ending of its own, I now see.

Twenty years later I sit with my patients and listen to their stories, trying to understand the certainly-marys and mixed-up courters of their lives, the unbearable desires and unspeakable fears—hoping I can make sense of it not twenty years hence but with them in the present as they try in their way to be free.

Funny how a person can become a bird; how a bird can be a human being.

5

The Day a Billionaire Walked into My Office

It was a rather ordinary Spring afternoon in New York City when I started a consultation with a young man who had called a few days prior seeking an appointment. Dressed in business casual, he looked his stated age, acted in a polite manner and spoke in a calm, muted tone. It was nearing my lunch break, and I admit that thoughts of what I would procure to satisfy my hunger flitted through my mind.

A few minutes into the session I learned that this patient was the co-founder of a well-known social media platform and . . . worth about one billion dollars. He was in his late twenties. I say "worth" not because the sum total of a person's character can be measured by a dollar amount but instead because if a tragedy suddenly befell him that is the approximate amount his beneficiaries would receive, or, less dramatically perhaps, if he decided to cash out everything he owned on the spot, he could pocket about a billion dollars upon leaving my modest office.

A few further minutes into the session, to this young wealthy man's credit, he said that he realized how well-off he was, that he never had to work another day in his life, and that he didn't understand how having so much money had impacted him. He stated he wanted to understand this. I replied that this seemed like a worthwhile area to explore.

But this is not a story about a billionaire and his money; it's a story about a psychoanalyst, money notwithstanding. I was almost twice as old as him and, needless to say, in my profession I would not earn in my entire lifetime a respectable fraction of his current worth. But I had, as an analyst, a therapy expertise that might be able to assist him in his journey of self-discovery. And my initial midday hunger for lunch was transformed into a curiosity to hear his story.

When I later told a colleague that I had had a consultation with a billionaire in his twenties, he replied, "I bet that stirred up your envy." This got me thinking. Honestly, during the consultation I was not aware of feeling envy. I was aware of some hopefulness that I would actually be able to charge this patient a full fee. He stated he did not want to use his insurance and he would pay privately. The fee would be less than a drop in the bucket for him, of course, but it would be helpful to me, given that more and more of my patients were using their insurance, which translated to lower and lower fees. But, again, contrary to my friend's comment, I was not cognizant of feeling envy for this patient because of his financial status. I don't know if, at the time, this was because I was defending against such intense envy or for some other reason. But I did think it was interesting that instead of feeling envy or resentment toward him, I was aware of the possibility that I might be able to help him and at the same time benefit financially from earning a fee I believed I was *worth*, given how much education and training I had completed to become an analyst. It was also true that the social media giant which he co-founded was not something I had ever used nor had any real interest in using, despite the fact that it was spreading like wildfire—or the plague, depending on your perspective—across the world. Yet, I became in the course of the hour more interested in it, how it was imagined and created, and its impact on society, no less *this* individual.

For I was just an analyst, in my office, day after day, trying to understand the unconsciouses of my patients and how to interpret them with them; trying to understand their transferences and my countertransferences and what it all means. I wasn't on social media; I wasn't playing with apps. I was clearly behind the times. A dinosaur, you might say. Still practicing psychoanalysis, a treatment over a hundred years old with barely any respect in society outside of my small circle of fellow analysts, an island entire of itself, hardly a piece of the continent or part of the main, as John Donne might have described our profession these days. A hundred years old seems a thousand times more than anything lasts anymore, given the speed with which technology is racing ahead.

So, then, how often does an analyst get to sit with a Dr. Frankenstein and discuss the "*monster*"? Perhaps I am overstating it, but the analogy I mean is to the sensitive Mary Shelley original version, not the distorted film version, of a brilliant scientist with high ambition to create something extraordinary and to the creation which may be tragically "misunderstood," as some literary scholars have suggested. My patient's "monster" has been, putting it not-too hyperbolically, taking over the planet, infiltrating people's lives in personal, professional, and, in a most recent notorious example, political ways unimagined until now. And, how often does an analyst sit with a patient in such a stark asymmetrical relationship financially? In the analytic literature recently it has been noted how difficult it is for patients to talk about money, mostly because of the shame, anxiety and embarrassment the topic brings. In fact, some have opined that it is harder nowadays for patients to talk about money than it is to talk about sex. In an effort to try to identify with this young man and his ungodly wealth, I reminded myself of the repeated finding that people who suddenly come into great wealth, such as winning the lottery, show an initial spike in reported happiness, but over time their curve of happiness settles back down to pre-wealth levels: So in the long-term the acquisition of great wealth does not increase reported happiness in life, after all. (Perhaps this thought, actually, was the defense against my unconscious envy, after all! Where is Melanie Klein when I need her!)

Nevertheless, in reflecting back upon my time with this man, I can't deny that I would have liked to have had the opportunity to try to prove that finding invalid for me. When I think of what I might have done with all that money. . . . But, wait, that's what everybody says!

Now, many years later, it turns out I'm still a working analyst and I still do not use this man's invention. His company is even more valuable now than it was when I saw him, but the company is also under increasing pressure and scrutiny from various corners and backlash from the public. There is some pushback. For every force there is an equal and opposing force, it seems. My former patient, lucky for him, had sold his shares in the company, so his wealth was secured. Interestingly, he had used his wealth to move on to other creative pursuits, developing projects and fulfilling aspirations distinct from the original lark that started in a college dorm which made him superordinately rich. My understanding is that this has led to mixed results thus far, including some business failures but also some highly innovative ventures. And he keeps working, even though he doesn't have to, as he once told me.

And, here I am, still analyzing, trying to make a living and support a family in an expensive city, trying to practice the treatment model I believe in and which continues to fascinate me, most of the time, and trying to engage patients, young like this man was and old now like me, in an exploration of how their minds work, how they could try to know themselves better, know better even the parts of themselves they would rather wish not to know.

I still wonder occasionally how this young man, now close to middle age, is doing, from an intrapsychic perspective, that is. I catch glimpses of his public and professional life from time to time in the news. I don't know what his net worth is anymore. I hope I know what my net worth is, not measured in dollars and cents.

Returning to that first session, instead of being aware of feeling envy, I do remember a humorous quote which came to mind. Dorothy Parker once said, "If you want to know what God thinks about money, look at the people He gave it to." (Perhaps another defensive thought!) Well, I don't really believe God had anything to do with this young man acquiring so much money so early on and seemingly so easily. He obviously had, with his co-founders, a groundbreaking idea and exceptional talent to bring the idea to fruition and then monetize it. But I also think about the same young men and women, his age with his education, for example, who were at that time my children's elementary school teachers earning about $40,000 a year. Broken down, that's about how much my patient made every three minutes during the work week.

So, yes, I do think something is askew in society, given the significance of the role those dedicated teachers played in the lives of our children, their relative lack of remuneration for it, and the inarguably gratuitous reward my patient made for helping to create the socially suspect behemoth smothering the globe. But, then, not surprisingly, when my children got older, they too wanted to use the damn thing my patient had invented, like all their friends, and, as it turned out, their teachers as well. Like I said, I'm a dinosaur. Perhaps even worse, a Luddite, since there was nothing bad about the poor dinosaurs who lived for much longer than humans so far and became extinct through no fault of their own and Luddites were probably more resistant to progress than even their ancestors, the dinosaurs.

It turned out, as it were, that my patient evidently only wanted a consultation and not actual treatment. Maybe he wasn't ready for it, maybe he wasn't troubled or curious enough about himself. Maybe I wasn't the right therapist for him—who knows. But I also wonder about the dynamics of *anyone* working with him. That is, the dynamic of him going to a therapist for help at the same time the reality of the economic inequality existing between him and his therapist, that he could buy out any therapist or analyst a billion times over. How does one address, if at all, that disparity in the treatment? It would seem to me it would have to be addressed at some point, otherwise it remains a dinosaur in the room. The fact that we did not have the opportunity to discuss it, nor to explore what he stated in the first appointment as his desire to better understand the impact of his wealth, remain for me the unanswered billion-dollar questions. The fact that I did not have the opportunity, in working with him, to make my unconscious envy more conscious and deal with it in the service of understanding him, remains for me the unanalyzed billion-dollar dynamic.

I happen to think that psychoanalysis, imperfect as it is, is still the best method we have to tackle such billion-dollar questions and to elucidate such unconscious dynamics. I recall a character in a David Mamet movie saying, "Everybody needs money. That's why they call it *money*!" A humorous tautology, but while I don't think everyone needs to be in analysis, I do believe everyone, including me, could use, at least, a little *analysis*.

6

A Portrait of the Analyst as a Young Man

Et ignotas animum dimittit in artes.
("And he turned his mind to unknown arts.")
— Ovid, Metamorphoses, VII, 188,

Epigraph to James Joyce's *A Portrait of the Artist as a Young Man*

"Once upon a time and a very good time it was . . ."[1]

Standing on the psychoanalytic precipice, looking out at the horizon, the young analyst sees an *obscure object of desire*. The sea horizon is the straightest line in nature, but the through-line from Freud's creation of psychoanalysis to the present day feels like a bend in the space-time continuum.

---

[1] This quote and the subsequent quotes immediately following the temporal headings are borrowed from Joyce (1916).

Revolutionary at the beginning, one hundred years of fortitude, the future appears ever more quixotic.

The young analyst asks himself, Where am I? How did I get here? Where am I going? Where is psychoanalysis going? (It feels like a dream. . . .) He tries to understand, but can at first only remember memories, fragments of experience, parts of himself like sea shells washed upon the shore. He believes that exploring himself in the third person, like young Stephen Dedalus, affords him both closeness and distance to both experience and observe—to be both subject and object of analysis.

Past

"The past is consumed in the present and the present is living only because it brings forth the future."

As the child of an analyst, having completed analytic training, having experienced two separate analyses, and working as a practicing analyst, the young analyst feels psychoanalysis is both known and unknowing to him. He always feels he is not only being but also becoming an analyst at the same time (Kravis, 2017). While he knows what he knows and he believes what he believes about what psychoanalysis is and what it isn't, psychoanalysis is a living document that he rewrites in each new analysis with each new patient—a lived experience that is created and re-created in analysis with every human being. Like rivers, you never step into the same analysis twice. Ever-present yet elusive, it is life-sustaining yet something which brings him, like others, closer to his own mortality (Poland, 2016). A well-spring of insight into the mind, it tests the limits of his knowledge and his own subjective mind. If you look out into space, you know it goes on forever, but you can only see so much in your field of vision, and you can hardly comprehend infinity. One thing he does know: The analyst analyzes, *ad infinitum*.

As a youngster, the young analyst suffered a sports injury which kept him mostly on his back in bed for months. Deprived of playing the game he loved, to stave off depression and loneliness, he started to read, this time with purpose. He became the boy who couldn't stop reading. Literature was his balm. And then he found Freud, out of curiosity pulling down the *Standard Edition* off his mother's bookshelf. Freud is meant to be discovered at an impressionable age. He discovered Him in a vulnerable state. He remembers reading and trying to understand "The Interpretation of Dreams" and "Three Essays on the Theory of Sexuality." He remembers comprehending not much of what he read. But in a strange way he felt a brave new world opened up to him, as he was mourning the loss of his prior identity and entering the *sturm und drang* of adolescence. A seed had been planted in his mind about the mind. And an unconscious identification with his analyst-mother which set him on his course.

In college, his favorite professor was an Aristotle philosopher who had told him that originally he had wanted to be a psychoanalyst but that would mean he could work only with one person at a time. He wanted to reach more people, so he became a teacher, and he tried to reach the minds of many young students. He also said that students are mistaken in thinking that they are there to learn from the professors. It's really the other way around: The professors are there to learn from the students, he said.

When the young analyst wondered about a possible future career for himself, he thought:

Some people study things.
I want to study the people who study things.

So first he became a psychologist.

During his first week of graduate school, he got a haircut on the university campus. The barber looked at him in the chair and muttered, "So, are you a freshman?" Feeling demeaned, he replied, "No, actually I'm getting a Ph.D. in psychology." The barber snapped back, "Uh oh, now I'm going to have to watch what I say!" Hurt, for some inexplicable reason an old Barbra Streisand song popped into his head and he said, "Just think of us as 'people who like people.' " As soon as it came out of his mouth he couldn't believe he had said that, but the barber spent the next half hour, scissors in hand, telling him his life story. That was his first effective clinical intervention, but he could never listen to Barbra Streisand songs again.

The young analyst remembers standing outside the classroom for what felt like an eternity after defending his doctoral dissertation, seven years in the making, as his committee conferred inside. His advisor finally opened the door and said, "Congratulations, Dr.—!" He remembers nearly fainting. He remembers afterward his classmate buying him clam chowder, fish and chips, and ale in the middle of winter to celebrate—this was New England!—and then on his tipsy way home thinking to himself, "Ah, so what do I do now?"

But of course there were plans to make, jobs to take, claims to stake in the real world. There were bills to pay, student loans to repay, romances to play. But: Practicing psychotherapy for him needed to go deeper. How to dig deeper? How to under-stand at a deeper level? What is *deep,* anyway?

He remembered the closing lines of a Robert Frost (1939) poem:

> I have a mind myself and recognize
> Mind when I meet with it in any guise
> No one can know how glad I am to find
> On any sheet the least display of mind.

In his mind he played with the poem and substituted "couch" for Frost's "sheet." The privilege to take up residence in another's mind: *One must dwell in the house of the mind.* Psycho-analysis held out the promise of a theory of the mind, a research into the mind, and a technique to heal the mind's suffering. Yes, a life of the mind. And for him, it included a fourth dimension: The wish to recapture the ability to wonder like a child and play in the playroom of the unconscious.

So then he became a psychoanalyst.

During one of his interviews for analytic training, the senior analyst sat down to start the interview and declared, "I'm here to find out what your neurosis is." He wondered if he knew what he was getting himself into by applying for analytic train-ing! He finished the interview not knowing if the analyst had found his neurosis. He wasn't sure himself what his neurosis was. But he felt the analyst was an interesting man and proba-bly a good analyst. This was an analyst who would dare to ask, "Is there life without mother?" on the cover of a book. Yes, he thought proudly, analysts ask such questions. And given his own history, he would need to try to answer this question.

When his first training case was approved, his supervisor said, "Let us hope this young woman has the fortitude to take advantage of the life-changing opportunity you have to offer her." When his second case was approved, his second supervisor said, "Great! We'll have fun."

These two comments, juxtaposed, captured for him what training could be about, what learning could be about, and what *analysis* could be about: "life-changing" and "fun" can be strange bedfellows. It reminded him of other juxtapositions and paradoxes, like the young Marine in Stanley Kubrick's (anti) Vietnam War film, "Full Metal Jacket" who's helmet has the words "Born to Kill" written on it while on his body armor is a peace button. When interrogated by the Colonel about what this means, the Marine replies, "I think I was trying to suggest something about the duality of man, Sir, the Jungian thing," to the Colonel's dumbfounded stare. Born to kill and peace symbol. Eros and Thanatos. A lifetime of analytic work lay ahead of him. . . .

The young analyst remembers a Freud class on "*Three Essays on the Theory of Sexuality.*" While the instructor was explicating the unique place that the sexual instincts hold in the psyche, the instructor made the comment, "There's something special about sex." He thought he saw a twinkle in the instructor's eye! And for a moment he felt like that young boy again, lying on his injured back reading the "*Three Essays*" and not quite comprehending but feeling its effect. Intellectual understanding finally followed an emotional impact: A circle was rounded. "*And our little life/Is rounded with a sleep*" (Shakespeare, 1623).

The young analyst remembers graduating from training, his analytic heart in his hands, and wondering what he was graduating into. An institute of like-minded colleagues, a family of intellectual relatives, an association of fair representation and forward-looking leadership? Was he entering the psychoanalytic movement, which had been subversive, or the psychoanalytic establishment, which had become conservative? What was psychoanalysis now? Where was it going? Who did he want to be in it? And would he have a voice? How ironic, he came to think, how an endeavor that gives unparalleled license to the patient to say the unsayable has been organized to often muffle the voice of the young practitioner. Why has it been so difficult for candidates-in-training and junior analysts to freely speak their minds, in print or into the air?

He didn't understand the current appeal of much lauded notions in the field like theoretical "pluralism." The popular view of multiplicity of perspectives was overvalued, he thought, and without real critical analysis for fear of appearing authoritarian or overly conservative. It seemed pretty clear to him how the creator of psychoanalysis had defined psychoanalysis. And it looked to him that pluralism had unfortunately begotten tribalism in the discipline. He thought of Janis Joplin's lyric, *"Freedom's just another word for nothing left to lose."* He tweaked this in his mind to sing, *"Pluralism's just another word for nothing left to think."* He remembers a teacher telling him, "There's been a lot of psychoanalysis in the past hundred years since Freud," while in the next breath acknowledging that there is no consensus on what psychoanalysis is and how it should be practiced. He was dismayed about all the debates and discord over education, standards, certification, governance, etc. It seemed he was entering a field in such internal turmoil. Like he was on a Titanic sinking while the stewards rearrange the deck chairs. Even if it stayed afloat, it seemed to be sailing further and further away from its founder, its father.

And finally he became a father.

Having children changes everything. One can dwell in the house of the mind, but now one must also pay the rent for a growing family, change endless diapers, and stay home with terror in caring for a sick child, or two. Priorities shift. Demands increase. Nothing prepares one to be an analyst except practicing and experiencing analysis. But nothing prepares one to become a parent, least of all one's own childhood. But the parent can witness consciousness arising *in vivo* in his children and behold a more transparent unconscious. And the parent can recover the *"radical innocence"* (Yeats, 1921) necessary to learn from his children. The young analyst never tired of hearing his children calling him a "poo-poo" and laughing. He had used to believe that the role of a child is to grow up. But he came to realize that, actually, *the role of a child is to be a child.*

His children's normal developmental insecurities rekindled his own latent neurotic anxieties. On the way home from his daughter's first day of school, he asked her if she made some nice new friends, and she answered, "Yes, I just hope they like me again tomorrow!" Yes, my darling, he thought to himself, I hope everyone likes me again tomorrow too!

All the young analyst wanted was to be the best analyst—and the best father and husband—he could be. And he came to understand that the stability and comfort of family life freed him to explore in his work the darker sides of himself and his patients. Flaubert once said, *"Be regular and orderly in your life, so that you may be violent and original in your work."* Like the artist the analyst tries to embody this in order to be able to hold the psyche of another.

The analyst should be an artist. An artist of the mind.

And all along he hoped to be a humanist. While his training exposed him to the various theoretical schools of thought and technique, if anyone had the temerity to ask him what *kind* of analyst he was, he wanted to answer, "A humanist." But it occurred to him that this description is redundant. An analyst *is* a humanist. A humanist of the highest order. A humanist of the individual within the world. A humanist of the unconscious.

PRESENT

"To discover the mode of life or of art whereby your spirit could express itself in unfettered freedom."

It is a very different world now, the young analyst discovers. Different from the world of analysts of yore having wait lists of patients wanting analysis. Different from the world of patients of yore coming every day for years and wanting to pay for it. Different from insurance companies willing to reimburse for valued analytic treatments and not interfering. Different from analysis holding a respected place in intellectual, scientific, and medical circles. Different from analysis being the novel, preferred treatment for old-fashioned hysteria to new-found character disorder, for those with a capacity for self-reflection and a motivation to change who could engage with a desire to alleviate self-deception and know how one's own mind works. To transform neurotic misery into common unhappiness, as Freud thought. Or, perhaps the goal of analysis is not only to foster insight but also to help people live in more radiant darkness.

But now there are super-pharmaceuticals, short-term and no-term therapies, and mis-managed care ruling over us, the young analyst laments, there are smartphones, the internet, and virtual reality distracting ourselves from ourselves. The culture has changed. Most people would rather sit in front of their computers for hours on end than lie in front of an analyst for 50 minutes. The examined life seems not worth living. *"Turn on, tune in, drop out,"* takes on new meaning in an age of quick fixes, digital compulsion, and e-fetish. The *zeitgeist* has little interest in psychoanalysis and psychoanalysts. Why is analysis more mocked than revered, and relegated to cartoon characterization? He wonders if the center of psychoanalysis can hold, or if it will fall apart like so many antiquated relics around it.

> The young analyst is in a subway car surrounded by cellphone zombies staring down at their illuminated screens. He is walking down the street dodging the walking dead staring down at their illuminated screens. He sits in a cafe staring at the automatons staring at their illuminated screens, imprisoned in their techno-autistic bubbles. Even in his office during sessions his patients' phones start ringing, their texts start pinging, and they stare down at their illuminated screens, as if possessed by the new *illuminati. People are wedded to their devices and homogenizing their experiences* (Kravis, 2017). He thinks: What have we become? Is all lost?

But then he remembers the line, *"What thoughts I have of you tonight, Walt Whitman,"* from Allen Ginsberg's (1956) poem and he feels a measure of comfort again, when simply walking through a supermarket and looking around could conjure such reverie. Maintain the wonder and curiosity of a child and the passionate sense-perception of a Whitman or a Ginsberg, he says to himself. Try to always be thinking like an analyst and feeling like a poet.

He is moved to reread from his notes over the years some of the remarkable things his patients have said to him.

"I know you are trying to save my life."

"Love means something you can't have."

"I have pain I can't make peace with."

"I was born with my heart on the wrong side."

"My coat needs therapy too."

"I only feel like a whole person if someone is looking at me."

"We're like floating minds on an abstract pool of water."

"I'm like a chameleon. I can be lots of different things but the one thing I can't be, that's me."

"I have no more stories to tell."

"I've accepted my relationship with the mirror."

"I can dress in layers of consciousness."

"I feel like I'm dancing between raindrops."

"My life is in search of a narrative."

"Silence makes me not be able to breathe."

"The more I love someone the more I hate them."

"My father might as well have been outlined in chalk."

"I feel like I'm uncovering the black iceberg of anger."

"My life is a near-death experience."

"I am not on the normal curve."

"I cannot accept the depth of my flaws."

"I am a movement without a cause."

"I dreamt I was being raped by a ghost."

"I'm wearing my therapy outfit."

"I wish I could create an app that would reconfigure my thinking."

"Nothing hurts when you can be somebody else"

"I'm looking for the answers in your carpet."

"I'm trying to be as honest as I can be without crossing into
dishonesty."

"I'm living like I'm dying."

"Life beat the pride out of me."

"The days crawl by, but the weeks fly by."

"I have shingles in my emotions."

"I'm a hot mental mess."

"I would like to put myself in every one of your books,
Dr.—"

"I'm a dead person's dream."

"I see pieces around me but I can't see myself."

"One day I'm going to get all my faculties together."

"We make plans and God laughs."

"If we didn't have shit, we would have to invent it."

"I'm a romantic masturbator."

"I want to light shit on fire."

"I know tomorrow can come and the earth could open up
and swallow me."

"I need to get out of my own way."

"The moments which are most real are when I'm staring at
the wall stone-faced."

"My life is like twisted metal."

"My being feels like a collection of wreckage from the past."

"I'm in a triangle and the corners are closing me out."

"I feel like I'm just renting space in my head."

"I'm sicker than my secrets."

"I never leave this room in my mind."

"As long as I have oxygen, I'll keep fighting."

The young analyst knows his patient-poets have put it better than he ever could. The quotes appear in his memory like fragments of people, of selves, like shells washed upon the shore and as he remembers the words of his patients the patients themselves come back to life for him, patients in full, and he becomes fuller to himself in reflection with them. Patients whose lives he hoped to have helped, who touched him in their *"irreducible subjectivity"* (Renik, 1993). People who exposed themselves and excoriated themselves, like he twice tried to, all their suffering, their resilience, their despair, their hopefulness, their inability to go on, their insistence to go on. Their wish to understand at odds with their fear of understanding. In short, their conflicted humanity. In the end, all humans have is their humanity.

The young analyst remembers that one of his first offices was in a nondescript building on a side street in New York City that made him feel he could be offering illegal back-alley abortions. In fact, he was offering *psychoanalysis*. He was full of pride and renegade pleasure to think he could help women—and men—who wanted their right to a psychological abortion and the pursuit of a psychoanalytic creation of their *own new life.*

Hours, days—years have passed in the analytic time-warp. Like dwelling in the house of the unconscious.

> In the room the patients come and go
> Talking of id, ego, and superego.

Future

"I go to encounter for the millionth time the reality of experience and to forge in the smithy of my soul the uncreated conscience of my race."

The young analyst wonders how similar his development has been to other analysts and how similar his future will be to those beyond him. He wonders if his ontogeny recapitulates the phylogeny of the field. Everyone is different, of course, all are unique. The journey to become an analyst is staked by individual histories and singular experiences and complex motivations. But no analyst is an island. All are part of the main, this community which communes in the analytic situation, birthed from humble origins with a curiosity of the mind, daring to be conquistadors in hostile times. Will the arc of his career bend toward the justice of most analysts? There are so many forces working against it, he thinks, is it possible to even think this *"unthought known?"* (Bollas, 1987). What would Freud say? Perhaps we reside in a *gotterdammerung* of psychoanalysis. When and what was the last truly great analytic idea? The young analyst resigns that such great ideas are beyond his reach and he wonders if there really are any more great ideas to be discovered or if we are really just dressing up old ideas in fashionable new clothes. There are limitless metaphors to explain analytic work. And, after all, doesn't everyone have a piece of the truth? One truth he has come to after practicing analysis for ten years is that no one should practice analysis until he or she has at least ten years of experience practicing analysis! But he wonders if there *is* an analyst hovering out there capable of such great heights again. And who has the voice to sound the clarion call? Where is the next shot across the bow? Where is the new spark to re-ignite the flame? A "second coming" (Yeats, 1920) for the field, as he, like most, strive toward simply achieving a personal best, a new analytic *becoming* with each new patient, enough patients to maintain a practice, enough practice to sustain a life. Hark, where is the next Freud? Alas, there will never be another Freud. But, pray tell, where *is* the next Freud?

He wishes there was more personal writing about our discipline, writing that would enliven how we communicate and humanize the work we do, to make contact with prospective patients, to reach our allied disciplines, to touch the public. He fears too often most are writing only to each other, at each other, because of each other. And yet, despite all the reports about its demise, the exaggerated reports of its death, the young analyst knows that psychoanalysis is still alive, still breathing oxygen, like his patient, to fight against the world's counterforces and to subdue the psyche's counterforces, because analysts are still analyzing, still pushing it forward, still paying it forward despite great odds with the conviction that good ideas will win out. Freud joked he was bringing The Plague though few people these days believe it could be The Cure. Our analytic project is great, but our analytic ambition should be modest. One must imagine Sisyphus, the happy analyst, repeatedly pushing a couch up the hill (Camus, 1955).

The young analyst remembers reading that Freud read more archeology than psychology. The young analyst reads more poetry than psychology. He notes how the poets have long staked our ground, from a different angle, with eloquence and concision and mystery. Before there was "field theory" (Baranger and Baranger, 2008), for example, there was Mark Strand (2002), field theorist:

> In a field
> I am the absence
> of field.

The line touches a nerve in the young analyst. What does it mean? Why do so many of his patients seem to be living this kind of "absence of field" life? Why can he feel at times it to be enclosing him? Where absence of field feels more real than presence. Why does it seem the field of psychoanalysis so often occupies an absence of field in the collective imagination?

It captures an aspect of the human condition that he must confront in himself, let alone his patients, let alone the world. Another poet, T.S. Eliot (1935), said, "*. . . human kind/Cannot bear very much reality.*" The young analyst believes the sentiment underpins the analytic theory of defenses. In short, like Eliot's Prufrock (1915), the young analyst is afraid, and he thinks at such times the only refuge is to turn to the poets. And the philosophers. He can imagine himself as an old analyst wearing, like Prufrock, his trousers rolled, if, that is, there is still analysis and if, that is, men still wear trousers! He imagines himself getting to the point—the hypothetical end-point of intellectual old age—where he can understand only metaphor, metaphor as the imaginary mindscape, the transitional literary space between fantasy and reality, between life and death:

> *"The owl of Minerva spreads its wings only with the falling of dusk."*

Hegel (1820), a Freudian before Freud, believed that full understanding, symbolized by Minerva, the Roman goddess of wisdom, is only possible when a historical phenomenon is concluded, when it has become part of the past. The young analyst sees each patient and himself as a potential Minerva lying on the couch trying to spread her wings to understand the past. Like Freud's *nachträglichkeit*.

In the modern world, or post-modern world, or post-post-modern world, or post-psychoanalytic world, the world spins too fast for most, for him, too. So many are left behind. Psychoanalysis tries to keep up. With each new invention, with each new technology, each new "app," the young analyst does not ask who will benefit from it. He asks rather who will suffer? Who will *suffer* from this? His patients are suffering from their own misbegotten pasts, the haunting of ghosts never freed to be ancestors, from an incomprehensible present, and a terrifying future. His leaning is with the most vulnerable, the disenfranchised souls, the marginalized minds, those living lives of *"quiet desperation"* (Thoreau, 1854). Of existences victimized by the *"slings and arrows of outrageous fortune,"* (Shakespeare, 1603) who cross the fearful threshold of his office door. The analyst is the purveyor of lost causes *par excellence,* including the lost cause of his own noble profession. But, unlike Marc Antony, *I come to praise psychoanalysis, not to bury it!*

End

"Old father, old artificer" —dead Freud—*"stand me now and ever in good stead."*

The young analyst steps down from the precipice and . . . He thinks of Joyce, the model for his *kunstlerroman,* he thinks of Freud, the model for his analytic thought, then he thinks of all his analytic forefathers and foremothers, including his own analyst-mother, whose work paved the way for him to work, then he thinks of the poets and the philosophers searching for truth and meaning in their own time and their own place against their own undoing and he thinks of his own analytic elders, of his teachers and his supervisors, and their late-career generation as they face the ultimate challenge of their impending mortality, as he thinks of himself and his generation of struggling and striving young analytic brethren analyzing against the fierce winds of resistance along the psychoanalytic diaspora of this most improbable of professions toward mid-career trying to preserve analysis for themselves and for the next generation, the as-yet unborn psychoanalysts slouching towards Bethlehem or Vienna or Dublin or New York or . . . to be born.

REFERENCES

Baranger, M. & Baranger, W. (2008). The analytic situation as a dynamic field. *International Journal of Psychoanalysis* 89:795–826.

Bollas, C. (1987). *The Shadow of the Object: Psychoanalysis of the Unthought Known*. New York: Columbia University Press.

Camus, A. (1942). *The Myth of Sisyphus and Other Essays*. New York: Vintage, 1991.

Eliot, T. S. (1915). The Love Song of J. Alfred Prufrock. In *T. S. Eliot: Collected Poems, 1909–1962*. New York: Harcourt Brace, 1991.

Eliot, T. S. (1935). Burnt Norton. In *T. S. Eliot: Collected Poems, 1909–1962*. New York: Harcourt Brace, 1991.

Hegel, G. W. F. (1820). *Elements of the Philosophy of Right*. United Kingdom: Cambridge University Press, 2017.

Frost, R. (1939). A Considerable Speck. In *The Poetry of Robert Frost: The Collected Poems*. New York: Henry Holt, 1979.

Ginsberg, A. (1956). A Supermarket in California. In *Allen Ginsberg: Collected Poems 1947–1997*. New York: Harper, 2007.

Joyce, J. (1916). *A Portrait of The Artist As a Young Man*. New York: Penguin, 1985.

Kravis, N. (2017). The googled and googling analyst. *Journal of the American Psychoanalytic Association* 65:799–818.

Poland, W. (2016). Slouching towards mortality: Thoughts on time and death. *Journal of the American Psychoanalytic Association* 64:795–802.

Renik, O. (1993). Analytic interaction: Conceptualizing technique in light of the analyst's irreducible subjectivity. *Psychoanalytic Quarterly* 62:553–571.

Shakespeare, W. (1603). *Hamlet*. New York: Simon and Schuster, 2012.

Shakespeare, W. (1623). *The Tempest*. New York: Simon and Schuster, 2016.

Strand, M. (2002). Keeping Things Whole. In *Mark Strand: Collected Poems*. New York: Knopf, 2014.

Thoreau, H. D. (1854). *Walden*. Hollywood, FL: Simon and Brown, 2011.

Yeats, W. B. (1920). The Second Coming. In *The Collected Poems of W. B. Yeats*. New York: Scribner, 1996.

Yeats, W. B. (1921). A Prayer for My Daughter. In *The Collected Poems of W. B. Yeats*. New York: Scribner, 1996.

7

SUBWAY ODYSSEY
IN TRUMP TOWN

I am on the subway in New York City, the hometown of President Trump. I stand here looking at all the people riding in this car with me, people of all different nationalities, races, religions, languages, personal histories and traumas, values and beliefs. Perhaps nowhere else is there as dense a representation of people from all walks of life. It occurs to me that we are, all of us, refugees in the human condition. I watch as everyone is doing what they all do on the subway every day: Some are reading, some are listening to music, some are talking with each other, many, as is the case these days, are staring down at their phones writing email or texting or playing video games, and a few, like me, are looking around too. The subway is one of the most democratic places on earth: There is no reserved seating, no first class, business class or coach, no VIP treatment. Everyone pays the same fare (some have slight discounts, of course, like seniors) and everyone gets the same service—no matter who you are. But you would never know by looking around a random subway car moving in a linear direction underground through the bedrock of a city in the middle of a summer evening, that, as W. B. Yeats said, we are "Turning and turning in the widening gyre/ The falcon cannot hear the falconer;/ Things fall apart; the center cannot hold;/ Mere anarchy is loosed upon the world,/ The blood-dimmed tide is loosed, and everywhere/ The ceremony of innocence is drowned;/ The best lack all conviction, while the worst/ Are full of passionate intensity."

Yeats wrote these lines in 1919, from his poem "The Second Coming," in the aftermath of the First World War, but they echo in my mind as we roar through a tunnel at full speed deep below the island of Manhattan. You would never know that *something* more serious and frightening and insidious than perhaps most of us could have imagined—an internal war—is unfolding above ground in this city, in Washington, D.C., all around this country, and reverberating around the world.

I don't know if President Trump has taken the subway in the recent past, or ever did in all the years he lived in this city before moving to our nation's capital to assume the most powerful and influential position in the world. But as I ride through the city's bowels I feel like I am traversing through the dark caverns of a pathological mind I cannot see through to the light. A strange, unfathomable interior devoid of reason, logic, honesty, maturity, compassion. The subway is falling apart, we are told in daily newspaper articles. The system is in crisis. America is falling apart, our commentators tell us. Our democracy is under assault, from *within*. The world is in disarray. So many people are suffering so much. "Because of an earlier incident . . ." has become the ubiquitous preface to announce that the trains are suspended or running with delays. You could almost re-imagine this announcement as, "Because of an earlier incident, Donald J. Trump is the President of the United States."

When I was a kid I used to love to ride in the subway. It was fast. It was full of interesting-looking people. It made a lot of noise. Sometimes it would halt momentarily in the middle of the tunnel, sometimes the lights would flicker on and off, sometimes it would creep along at a snail's pace. But then it would barrel ahead again at top speed. I used to think subways went faster than cars or airplanes. I felt a child's pleasure simply in the experience of being on a subway journey. You could travel the entire city in it, like a modern day Odysseus, wandering through all the boroughs and their neighborhoods with their unique cultures, peoples, challenges, temptations, and seductions. And you could do it without much fear. But that was my age of innocence. I used to hum the melody and hear the words of Betty Comden and Adolph Green's great song, "New York, New York" from "On The Town": "And people ride in a hole in the ground!" Now it feels more like a hole in the head. Now the subway is no fun. Now you have to be hypervigilant: *If you see something, say something.*" Danger can strike anywhere. It's all about just getting where you have to go as quickly as possible and unscathed. It's far more expensive, far too crowded, too often delayed and derailed, and, perhaps worst of all, far too uncivil. So much so that the transit authority has to run ad campaigns encouraging riders to be courteous and considerate toward each other. Now feels like an "age of implosion": We are destroying ourselves from the inside out. Certainly there are real external threats, but the internal ones of distrust, paranoia, anger, hatred, incivility, and selfishness may be more deadly. Which brings my mind back to Trump. How have we come to this point where a person like Trump is president? What does he reflect about ourselves? Our land? Our moment in history? Our humanity—or inhumanity—toward each other? Is Trump just an aberration in the White House or the outgrowth of a metastasizing disease?

I don't know, but some of my patients have their own theories and they may talk about them when I see them today. Or they may just sit there and cry, which is what one patient did the entire session the day after Trump won the election. Never before in my practice has politics entered into the clinical hour as much as it has currently. But it's not so much politics, per se, as it is this *new* politics, this new *politician*, this "person" now occupying the White House. Not all of my patients talked about their feelings during the presidential campaign, or after the election, or even during the ensuing weeks and months of the new administration. This was, actually, remarkable in itself that some of them didn't bring it up at all. I could only understand it, at the time, as defensive: Repression, or a self-protective reaction to trauma. There was also an element of self-absorption, perhaps narcissism, in sitting down in my office and immediately returning to well-worn territory without so much as mentioning the dramatic election or the startling things taking place over the subsequent months. But patients sometimes do this. I did have one patient, a white male, with whom I had been working for several years and thought I knew pretty well, who surprised me when I learned he was supporting Trump and planning to vote for him. Obviously, it was not my place as his therapist to debate with him politics or, regarding this candidate, question his competence or even morality with the patient. I had to be careful not to let my own views seep out, no less my dumbfoundedness about his support for Trump, but instead keep my analytic stance and try to place his support for Trump in the context of what he and I were working on in the treatment and understand the meaning of all this. Then, slowly over time, it was striking to see how his view of Trump changed and how he changed his opinion as events unfolded, so much so that he regretted having voted for Trump and no longer supported him. Much of his change of mind was the result of the influence of his fiancé, a woman and a Democrat, who helped him see Trump in a different light, particularly his misogyny.

Nevertheless, for every one person like this patient, there are all those other people who haven't changed their minds about Trump, who haven't changed their minds about all the noxious beliefs that people like Trump espouse, who haven't ever changed their minds about things or anything about themselves. And this is where so much of the challenge for me arises in psychotherapy and psychoanalysis: Trying to help people reflect upon themselves and to question their beliefs, values, thought patterns, and to change, hopefully for the better. At times with patients and with myself as well it feels daunting because so much is so deep-seated. I remember Warren Poland's definition of psychoanalysis: "The systematic study of what you don't want to know about yourself." Helplessness in the face of the internal forces within our own minds, no less the larger forces in society, can take root and stubbornly not let go.

For I am just one New Yorker, one American, one Earthling, a former patient myself and now a practicing psychoanalyst, feeling powerless against the greater forces of Washington, other countries, unknown worlds. Sometimes I think the only thing that would unite everyone, that would allow everybody to put aside their differences and come together would be if our planet was attacked by alien invaders from outer space. . . . But, as a New Yorker, as an American, as an Earthling, and as an analyst, I have to believe that this subway will come to a stop at the next station, that there is light at the end of this tunnel, that this long national nightmarish ride of a presidency will cease at some point. Because the alternative, helplessness and depression, is a dead end. I have to believe that I and you will make it to work and back home today safely and sanely. That the whole system will improve. That the madness will end. That order and decency will be restored. That the center will hold. That Odysseus did not travel all that way and endure all that much to come home having learned nothing. That the falcon will hear the falconer once again. That we don't need aliens to save ourselves from ourselves.

8

THE NIGHT AN ANALYST COULDN'T SLEEP

I

It was the longest night I can remember. The night I couldn't sleep. I lay in bed thinking about this and thinking about that. Thoughts flitted through my mind as if I were reviewing my life up to that point and then trying to project into my future. I didn't feel troubled, at first, necessarily, by it all. Mostly just curious and struck by the feeling that my mind was working on its own, outside of my control. Of course, this is almost a contradiction in terms, if not an outright one, to think that my mind was working out of my control while at the same time I was observing what seemed to be going on within my control. Almost like I was experiencing something *and* observing it at the same time. But I don't want to get too "intellectual" about this; I want to try to stay with the feeling of it. As I say this I remember that's what my analyst used to remind me of. My second analyst, that is. My first analyst had started this line of analysis. I recall one hour in particular years into the analysis when, during a long patch in which I was describing something, knowing my family's background in the performing arts, he quoted the old saw, half-jokingly, "OK, now once more with feeling!" I think we had a short laugh. Then I tried again. My second analyst, during another long analysis years later, dispensed with the humor and told me straight away what I was doing, probably thinking it was about time we got somewhere with it.

Two analysts, two analyses, then years later a sleepless night. . . . Since I, too, was an analyst, it demanded that I do something about it, like think about it. And maybe not fight it. So, instead, I got up and went to my computer and tried to write about it. Why do people write? One person once said, "I write to know what I think." And why do people have sleepless nights? Elizabeth Hardwick wrote a novel, "Sleepless Nights," in which she reflected upon her life. But, again, this was *my* life and *my* sleepless night so I had to reflect upon *my life*, despite taking whatever small comfort in knowing someone else some other time had self-reflective sleepless nights and evidently something productive came out of it.

This sounds like something a good ego psychologist might espouse: Don't fight it; make something productive out of it. And I want to believe I am a good ego psychologist. And a good Freudian too, the best of what Freud offered. And that's why I tried to let my associations take me wherever they would and I was reminded of when I was a young boy playing tennis with fantasies of being a champion one day. One afternoon I was playing a match during a very windy day and getting increasingly frustrated. I couldn't control the ball. My timing was off and I could barely hit the ball in the direction I intended because the wind took it somewhere else. Suddenly, out of nowhere it seemed, I said to myself, "Make the wind your friend." And I repeated this to myself a number of times throughout the rest of the match, like a mantra. Or, now I think, like a helpful ego psychological intervention! The line made sense to me back then and still does now. There was no point in trying to fight the wind. It was a losing battle. I had to try to use the wind to my advantage; maybe adjust my strokes better to adapt to it. Hit the ball with less topspin and instead hit flatter. "Make the wind your friend." I don't remember if I actually played any better after this insight; perhaps a little. I don't remember if I actually won the match or not. Probably I didn't; I vaguely recall the other boy being a stronger player. But I think, about forty years later, that I became less frustrated on the court in dealing with the uncooperative wind. I may, in fact, have enjoyed myself a little more. I may have become more playful, I may have had more *fun*, which is what playing a game should be, especially as a child, instead of an overly competitive win-or-die task of torture, which is what it had become in my own mind. Imagine that, I have this recollection through an association and come to this realization, so many years later and so many miles away. It made me feel plaintive for my youth, but yet also uplifted at the same time. Two different feelings coming together during a sleepless night.

Years after I became an analyst I came across a passage in Sandor Ferenczi's *Clinical Diary* in which he recalled how he overcame a bout of seasickness by "synchronizing" his "will" with "that of the boat." Ferenczi used his personal experience as an analogy in discussing the idea of a "friendly acceptance of illness," that is, not fighting pain but rather allowing it to "run its course." And still years later Sheldon Bach in a paper referred to Ferenczi's seasick experience as an example of a "successful surrender and acceptance of a higher power" by not "fighting his fear and nausea" but rather trying to "attune himself with the waves." Waves for Ferenczi and for me as a child the wind. Now, the wind of a sleepless fear. . . .

II

On this night I couldn't sleep, my wife and children were sleeping soundly. I could hear them breathing. I could see them dreaming, but I couldn't see their dreams. They couldn't see me standing over them looking at them. They were in their own worlds, completely in their own minds. Their reclined bodies lying motionless in their beds, their consciousnesses far from me. These sleeping, dreaming bodies in front of me, unaware of my existence in the moment, were my loving family, and, along with my consciousness separate from them, my life separate from them, the sum of my life. But then, I can't really say anything *separate* from them because they are always with me, in a way, in my mind, always a part of me. I guess that's what being attached to others means, in a psychic sense, in an emotional sense. So I had this thought on this sleepless night as I watched them sleep that they were using my sleep to sleep even deeper for themselves.

III

Being a psychoanalyst and believing in a psychoanalytic understanding of how the mind works didn't prove to be any aid in getting me to sleep on this night, yet. In fact, maybe it worked more against it, at first. I remember a clinical supervisor, a senior analyst with whom I worked during my analytic training, who once explained to me that some children may have difficulty falling asleep because of the difficulty, as he put it, of "leaving one world and entering another." What he meant, of course, was the experience of leaving wakefulness, of conscious awareness, and entering unconscious sleep, the world of dreaming, the world of primary process and the dynamics of Freud's dream-work. So this night, I thought, I was like a child again, resisting sleep, resisting dreaming, staying awake to protect myself from entering the world of my unconscious mind. But what could I have been afraid of *this* night in going to sleep? Of dreaming? What was different *this* night, out of all the others? I didn't know; I may never know.

IV

It was getting even later in the night, or, rather, earlier in the morning. I couldn't tell when the night became the morning. Maybe I couldn't tell where I started and where I stopped, where wakefulness ended and sleep started, or vice versa. Boundaries felt blurry to me. Without boundaries how can one tell anything apart? Maybe we can only know something through contrasts. The contrast I was presently struggling with was my increasing need to sleep against my apparent inability to sleep in the moment. As if there were two forces at odds with each other. Conflict. I was in conflict. Perhaps I am a conflict theorist, after all. Whatever I am, I was tired, and maybe I shouldn't fight it, but rather make the tiredness my friend. Sort of like what some contemporary analysts mean when they advise not to fight against the resistance, the way they think Freud espoused, but rather to "roll with the resistance." But, in my case, this night, there was a difference between being tired and being sleepy. My body was tired but my mind was active. That was my Cartesian split this night.

V

It's a strange thing to be an analyst in this day and age. There are so many pressing things going on in the world, it feels at times almost overwhelming. What possible impact can psychoanalysis have anymore, I wonder . . . ? Most people seem to think, if they knew anything about us to begin with, that we died a slow, lonely, unremarkable death some time ago. We died a whimper, not a bang. When I started analytic training I was searching for a larger office in which I could fit an analytic couch. One office owner said to me, "You need space for a couch? I thought no one practiced analysis anymore." And this was a psychiatrist on the faculty of a major teaching hospital in New York City! But the analysts who still exist, young and old, still practice, still analyze against so much resistance in society at large, including our own mental health field. I remember during one hour in my own analysis, my training analysis, my second analysis, when I must have been sounding plaintive again about all of this and my analyst, perhaps sensing that I needed some ego boosting or encouragement in the moment, expressed the belief that "Good ideas will win out." I took this to mean that despite all the forces opposing psychoanalytic thinking and practice, ideas that have value and truth will persevere and eventually be accepted and embraced. It was somewhat out of character for her to offer up such a non-neutral statement like this in an otherwise fairly "traditional" or "conservative" analysis, but it was helpful to me in the moment, and as is apparent, I still remember it as meaningful on a sleepless night ages later.

I try to remind myself that, despite how the world has changed since the heyday when analysis was much respected as a field of inquiry and a therapeutic treatment, and despite how fewer people seek out analysis, insurance companies won't pay for it, and the academy has little use for analysts on their faculties anymore, that analysis can still help certain people, that it can still be an effective treatment for the right kind of person, perhaps the *most* effective treatment for that right kind of person, and that its model of the mind may still be the best working theory of human psychology. In fact, in order to not get so discouraged about the state of our field, I have to remind myself that it is still me and the patient alone in the office working together hour after hour and day after day that matters most, away from everything else going on, everything else trying to subvert our progress. It doesn't matter how psychoanalysis is looked upon in the academy, how psychoanalysis is portrayed in the mass media, how the prejudice or the ignorance out there is opposing you—these are other challenges to confront, other battles to be fought—if your patient is making headway and analysis for *this* person at *this* time is working. If you are making a difference in this one person's life. That's it.

VI

Then, as night was stealthily turning into dawn, I realized that what I was most afraid of was not not sleeping this night but rather, actually, *not dreaming*. Yes, that was it. I had had near-sleepless nights before, and survived the next day relatively undamaged. But, now, for some reason, the thought of having a night without dreaming filled me with dread. How could I work the next day—how could I function!—without having at least one fully or half or marginally-remembered dream? How could I face the next day; how could I deal with my patients' unconsciouses without having faced my own unconscious the night before? Without confronting my own boiling cauldron of fear and desire? It seemed to me I had to meet the dream myself, engage the dream-work myself, play with the primary process, in order to tackle Sphinx-like riddles in others. I remembered reading that Oliver Sacks, an avid swimmer and explorer of the mind himself, once wrote:

> Swimming gives me a sort of joy, a sense of well-being so
> extreme that it becomes at times a sort of ecstasy. . . . The
> mind can float free, become spellbound, in a state like a
> trance. I have never known anything so powerfully, so
> healthily euphoriant—and I am addicted to it, fretful when
> I cannot swim.

Well, dreaming for me is like what swimming was for Sachs. Yes, now I understood, I could tolerate little or no sleep, but no dreaming?! I would feel incomplete the next day, lacking something, my mind deprived of something vital from the night before, my mind bereft. A night without dreaming, a night without conversing with my unconscious would leave me fretful the next day.

And with this realization, so very early in the morning, I began to feel sleepy. "To sleep, perchance to dream." I felt a calmness, an ease to enter into that other world. It would be my dream, no one else's. A product of my own psychology. My creation. A masterpiece of mind.

I now wanted to go to sleep because I wanted to dream. I would be seeing patients soon and my mind must be alert to their minds. My unconscious attuned to their unconscious. I wondered how they slept and what they dreamt this past night while I sat up thinking about them, about my family, about myself, about psychoanalysis, as I too finally drifted off to sleep and into my other world. I thought of what my children like to say to me as they fall to sleep, "See you in dreamland, Daddy," and I was no longer afraid too.